HALLOWEEN PARADE

For Emma

PUFFIN BOOKS
Published by the Penguin Group
Penguin Books USA Inc., 375 Hudson Street, New York, New York 10014, U.S.A.
Penguin Books Ltd, 27 Wrights Lane, London W8 5TZ, England
Penguin Books Australia Ltd, Ringwood, Victoria, Australia
Penguin Books Canada Ltd, 10 Alcorn Avenue, Toronto, Ontario, Canada M4V 3B2
Penguin Books (N.Z.) Ltd, 182-190 Wairau Road, Auckland 10, New Zealand

Penguin Books Ltd, Registered Offices: Harmondsworth, Middlesex, England

First published in the United States of America by Viking Penguin,
a division of Penguin Books USA Inc., 1992
Published simultaneously in Puffin Books
Published in a Puffin Easy-to-Read edition, 1994

1 3 5 7 9 10 8 6 4 2

THE LIBRARY OF CONGRESS HAS CATALOGED THE PUFFIN BOOKS EDITION UNDER
CATALOG CARD NUMBER 92-60109.

Puffin Easy-to-Read ISBN 0-14-037143-5

Printed in the United States of America

Puffin® and Easy-to-Read® are registered trademarks of Penguin Books USA Inc.

Reading Level 1.6

HALLOWEEN PARADE

Harriet Ziefert
Pictures by Lillie James

PUFFIN BOOKS

Everybody has a lot to do
before Halloween.

And so does Allie.

A lot to do
A lot to do
A lot
A lot
A lot to do!

A costume...

A cape...

A mask...

Trick-or-treat bags
are important, too.

Everything is ready
for Halloween.

It's bedtime on the night
before Halloween.

It's hard to sleep.

Then it's morning.
And it's Halloween!

A lot to do

A lot to do

A lot
A lot
A lot to do!

Hurry! Hurry!

Hurry to school
for the Halloween parade.

See the ghosts.
See the goblins.

See the pumpkins.

Where's Allie?

Trick-or-treat!

Trick-or-treat!

Happy Halloween!